STARBOUND

J.J. GREEN

BOOK ORDER

The Books of Shadows of the Void - Complete Series

Prequel: Starbound
Book 1: Generation
Book 2: Stranded
Book 3: Dawn
Book 4: Shadowrise
Book 5: Underworld
Book 6: Burned
Book 7: Trapped
Book 8: Mars Born
Book 9: Shadow Battle
Book 10: Shadow War
Books 1 - 3 The Galathea Chronicles
Books 4 - 7 The Earth Chronicles
Books 8 - 10 The Galactic Chronicles

1

———

Jas Harrington gripped the handlebars of her snow mobile and pressed the throttle. The machine pulled away beneath her, sending up sprays of powder snow on either side. She grinned.

It had snowed the day before. The first snow that year, though winter was almost over. Maybe the last snowfall at low altitude on Earth forever, some said. Over the last few decades, Antarctica had changed almost beyond recognition as raised global temperatures melted its massive ice sheets, calving icebergs as large as countries to melt into the ocean.

At that moment, Jas didn't care what humans had done to their home planet. She didn't feel as though Earth was *her* home anyway. She'd grown up on Mars until she was twelve and already weak-boned from the low gravity. When the paperwork came through from the Martian colonial government, she left the home for cared-for children and traveled to the mother planet to complete her adolescence at a second institution.

After months of aching muscles and headaches, her body had finally adjusted, but the policy of separating the Martian children for better 'integration' meant she'd been lonely. No one had told the Earth children they were supposed to let the newcomers integrate.

Sergei was riding his snowmobile parallel to hers as she powered over the ice, the roar of the engines making speaking impossible. A fellow student from the training college, his black hair streamed out from beneath his hat. Like hers, his eyes were hidden behind dark snow goggles. He waved at her and pointed in the direction they were heading. They had to be nearly at their destination, though she couldn't make it out against the snowy white landscape and the bright clouds.

She nodded in reply, and her heart surged. She didn't think she'd ever been this happy.

They were almost upon the igloo before she saw it. A crude lump of slightly dirty white became visible in the landscape. Sergei was already slowing down, and Jas did the same.

As they stopped and she stepped down from her vehicle, she smiled. The igloo was very clumsily put together, as if the builders had been drunk when they made it. Roughly cut blocks of ice balanced precariously upon one another, creating a haphazard wall. It looked like it would have fallen down if not for the freezing temperatures that seemed to be holding it together.

"This is it?" she asked.

Sergei was taking off his goggles. "Of course. How many other igloos do you think there are around here?"

Jas pulled off her goggles too, along with her hat and gloves. "But I thought you said it took you and Aaron two whole days to build it?"

"More than two days, if you include cutting the blocks." He took off his gloves. "Do I detect a tone of disbelief? I get it. It's hard to credit that we could construct such a magnificent edifice in such a short time."

"You're right." Jas tilted her head to take in the detail of the structure. "I...can't quite believe it." She couldn't hold in her laughter any longer. She burst into giggles and found she couldn't stop. She bent over, nursing her aching stomach. Pulling off her goggles to wipe her eyes, she finally began to catch her breath. "So *this* is what you meant by your Love Palace?"

Sergei frowned. "You dare to insult my Mansion of Delight? Be careful. You're treading on dangerous ground. I might have to remind you of something pretty important, now that we're out here in the snowy wastes, far from civilization and..." He went to the compartment of his snowmobile and reached inside. He pulled out a small battery-powered heater. "...warmth."

It was unusually cold that day, even for Antarctica. Jas's tears of mirth were already freezing on her cheeks. An icy wind had penetrated her snowsuit as they'd driven over, and she was chilled through. "Oh, come on. I was only kidding. It's a beautiful igloo. You and Aaron have some real talent. Let's go inside and warm the place up."

Sergei slowly shook his head. "I don't think so. I think I'll just go in by myself and get toasty, seeing as my Chateau of Sensation isn't good enough for your refined tastes. You can head on back to your dorm and cuddle up with your roomie instead. Maybe she's more your type." He winked at her.

"Don't be an idiot. Your Love Palace looks great. It really does. I don't know what I was thinking. I can hardly believe it only took you forty-eight hours to put it together. It would have taken me at least...I don't know..." She cast her gaze over the comical building. "Forty-eight minutes."

Sergei's fake frown had begun to disappear at Jas's apparent effort at reconciliation, and he'd raised the heater to hand it over, but upon hearing the end of her sentence he snatched it back. Jas made a lunge for the appliance, but Sergei sidestepped her, and she slipped and stumbled.

Laughing, Sergei ran to the other side of his snowmobile

and dangled the heater invitingly. Jas scrambled to her feet, slipping again twice, and reached across the vehicle. Sergei turned and sped away. Jas followed, and soon she was right behind him, her long legs carrying her quickly closer. He wasn't running fast, as if he wanted her to catch him. When she was almost there, Sergei skidded and tumbled down. Jas tripped over him.

The heater skittered across the ground, coming to rest a few meters away. Laughing, they crawled after it, grabbing at each other to slow the other down. Their breath plumed in the frigid air. Both were gasping as they fought to be the first to reach the heater. Jas lunged, and her fingertips brushed the appliance's edge where it lay upside down.

Sergei grasped her waist and dragged her backward, pulling her underneath him on the slippery surface. He tried to climb over her, but she turned on to her back and pulled him down. As they came face to face, they stopped struggling and their chuckles faded. Their warm, condensing breath intermingled.

Sergei's intense blue eyes were very close to Jas's. She felt herself disappearing into them. Sergei's muscles relaxed under her hands as they gazed at each other.

"That's *my* heater," she said softly.

"No, it isn't," he murmured. He leaned down to kiss her.

A few moments later, Jas wasn't cold any longer. The snow at the back of her head was melting and soaking her scalp in icy water, but she hardly noticed.

Sergei drew away from her. "Shall we go inside?"

Jas reached up and pulled his head down to hers again. "In a minute."

For many years, she remembered that day as the happiest day of her life.

2

———————

Four months earlier, Jas had arrived at the McMurdo Sound Training Institute fresh from her Earth children's home. The journey had been long—the meager amount of money she'd received when, at eighteen, she'd 'graduated' her care program hadn't stretched to a shuttle flight to the southern continent. She'd had to travel by old-fashioned airplane, and by the time she'd arrived she was exhausted.

When the autobus drew to a stop outside the two-story college, she was dozing. She only caught a glimpse of the prefab buildings before the bus pulled up. She disembarked, yawning, with the rest of the new students and collected her luggage from the compartment under the bus. Passing through opaque plexiglass doors, she went into the lobby.

The college wasn't much warmer inside than outside. Jas rubbed her arms as she stood in line waiting to register her arrival. The place was poorly lit and dank. It looked as though it hadn't been refurbished in the last thirty years, much like the areas of McMurdo Sound they'd passed through on the bus ride.

Jas was already regretting her decision to do the security training course, or at least her choice to do it at this remote location. She couldn't remember why she'd picked this college at the end of the world. The thought that she'd be spending the next three years here made her heart sink.

The line shuffled forward and Jas went along with it. The other students had their heads down, too tired or disinterested to begin making friends just then. Jas's nose was beginning to drip. She fished in a pocket for a tissue.

Her hand brushed a circle of plastic, and she pulled out the familiar object. It was a picdisk displaying rotating images of the friends she'd left behind when she came to Earth. Like her, the children were olive-skinned and their hair and eyes were reddish-brown. The coloring was common to all Martians—the gene therapy colonists received to help them survive the radiation altered skin and hair pigmentation. The effects were passed on to their offspring.

A feeling of nostalgia hit Jas, and she remembered what it had been about Antarctica that had appealed to her. She'd thought its climate and remoteness might be something like Mars, and she'd been right. Gnawing cold, low sunlight, and what seemed to be a grinding, survival nature to everyday life, did make the place like another planet. Antarctica already reminded her of her early childhood in the nearest thing she had to a home.

The line moved forward. Jas wondered why they hadn't automated the registration process. Did they want to see each student face to face? The others in the line were giving her glances. As always, her height and tell-tale skin and hair color betrayed her origins and attracted curiosity. The attention bothered her, though she'd grown a little used to it in the last six years. At least it prevented the necessity of answering questions about where she was from. Such questions always led to the awkward revelation that, as a young baby, she'd been the sole survivor of an infamous colony disaster.

The fact was a conversation killer, and as she had no memory of the incident and didn't like to even think about it, the information was something she preferred to keep quiet.

Another new student in the line was staring at her. The girl's curly brown locks were bulging out from under a thick hat she was still wearing even though they were now inside. Her face was round. She smiled at Jas, and deep dimples appeared on her cheeks.

Bemused by the girl's friendliness, Jas smiled back, a little half-heartedly.

The girl pointed at the line and rolled her eyes.

Jas wondered if she was making an embarrassing mistake, and that the girl was actually looking at someone behind her. She glanced over her shoulder, but the rest of those in the line were mostly engrossed in their hand held interfaces, reading, texting, or playing games. She was definitely the object of the strange girl's attention. Hesitantly, she smiled again.

A gap had opened up in front of her new acquaintance. Jas gestured at it, and the girl turned and moved up. She was almost at the desk, where three administrators sat, and in another moment she was in front of one and giving her details.

Jas took a final look at the picdisk displaying images of her old Martian friends before returning it to her pocket. She pushed her wheeled luggage forward with her toe as the line moved again.

JAS's ROOMMATE WAS A LONG-HAIRED, quiet girl called Aggy. When they met after registration, they said hello and put their things away. Aggy gave monosyllabic responses to Jas's efforts to be friendly. At dinner, she sat away from Jas and read her interface as she ate. Jas rolled her eyes and contented herself with filling her cold, empty stomach.

Classes started the following day. Jas's program was full. Combat training, fitness drills, weapons instruction and discipline, target practice, and survival training were compulsory. Battle tactics and leadership skills were two of the optional extras, and they were intended for students who wanted to make security a lifelong career, rather than use it as a cheap stepping stone to becoming a new world colonist. Working security aboard a colony starship was one way to avoid paying the fare, which cost many their life savings and more.

Other options included extraterrestrial life forms and zero and high gravity combat. Jas was taking all these and the career options. Though she wasn't eager to lead, she knew she would be bored if base-level security work turned out to be repetitive and undemanding.

After the first day, Jas flopped into an armchair in the shared living room of her dorm. She was physically tired but not exhausted. Though the training had been challenging, she'd exercised regularly for as long as she could remember—it was a mandatory aspect of Martian life to avoid some of the effects of low gravity—and her height gave her an advantage in hand-to-hand combat that made things easier for her.

She had half an hour to kill before dinner, and she wasn't sure what to do. She didn't want to go to the room she shared with Aggy. Her roommate was in a long-distance relationship, and maintaining it took up every spare moment she had. Whenever Jas saw her, she was having intense conversations with her far-away boyfriend, and at Jas's appearance she would drop her voice to a whisper, sometimes harsh, sometimes loving.

A door to another bedroom opened, and the girl who had stared at Jas in the line the previous day came into the living room. She'd finally taken off her hat. A near-Afro of brown curls framed her head. Her dimples reappeared.

"Hey, are you in room 239?" she asked.

"Yeah, that's right."

"I was wondering if it was empty. I didn't see you or your roomie at the dorm get-together last night."

"I didn't know there was one."

"Really? I put a note under everyone's door."

Jas wondered if Aggy had seen the note and not told her about it. "I didn't see it."

"And you didn't hear us?"

"I'd had a long flight, and I sleep pretty sound."

The girl held out her hand. "Tamara."

"Jas." They shook, and Tamara sat down.

"Sorry for staring at you in the line yesterday. It was a little rude of me. I was interested to see a Martian in real life."

"That's okay," Jas replied, tensing as she prepared for the inevitable personal questions.

But Tamara went on, "I'm studying colonial adaptation biology. You know, adaptive gene therapies and physiological and metabolic responses to extraterrestrial environments." Jas must have looked wary because she laughed and added, "Don't worry, I won't treat you like a test subject. I was just interested to meet you, that's all."

Jas relaxed a little. "I'm doing security training."

"Deep space program?"

"That's right."

"Extraterrestrials?"

"Yeah."

"Sweet. I'll wanna hear all about it. Hey, have you eaten yet?"

"No, it's too early." Jas winced a little as her words gave away that she had to eat in the cafeteria, which implied that she was a low-income scholarship student.

"It's never too early for my chili and rice. It's a secret family recipe. I invited some of the other girls, and you're welcome too."

"Thanks, I'd love to."

"How about your roomie?"

"I think she might have other plans."

3

Jas's opponent hit the mat with a thump, his eyes wide. For a moment, he lay there in shock, his exceptionally hairy arms and legs splayed out. Jas supposed that, at nearly the same height as her and a minimum of fifteen kilos heavier, he'd taken his victory in their sparring for granted. Over-confidence was a mistake only inexperienced fighters made. Jas's years of practice fighting bullies at her Earth children's home meant that she was far from inexperienced.

After a month of hand-to-hand combat training, Jas had sparred with all of her classmates, and the result had been the same every time. Each of them had ended up on the mat at her feet. After she'd worked her way through half the class, some didn't even try to fight. They threw half-hearted punches and slow kicks, as if only passing time while waiting for the inevitable conclusion.

"Get up," their instructor shouted at the defeated student. The young man got to his feet, but the instructor's eyes were on Jas. His name was Trankle, and he looked annoyed, though she had no idea why.

From his attitude and demeanor, it was obvious that Trankle was ex-military. He was bull-necked and strong-jawed, and his stance was awkward due to over-large muscles in his arms and legs. Jas had attracted more and more of the man's attention as the class went on. She guessed it was something to do with her beating everyone, but what was she supposed to do? Lose so that the others could feel good about themselves?

A movement to her side caught her eye, and she raised her arm just in time to parry a blow from her defeated opponent. Her forearm smashed into his, and the blow went wide, just missing the side of her head. Instead of leaving the mat, he'd tried to sucker punch her, only he hadn't gotten quite out of her range of vision.

Years of play yard fights and sneaky attacks from the worst of the Earth children's home inmates had honed Jas's reactions to muscle reflexes. Without thinking, she swung round with a fist, hitting the student square on the side of his face.

His head snapped around, and he staggered backward, dazed.

"Hey," Trankle shouted. In a couple of strides, he was at Jas's side and wrenching her arm behind her back, almost lifting her from her feet as he pushed upward and forward. Jas gasped in pain and tried to twist free.

"Aww, come on, man," said a student. "He deserved it." Others mumbled vague protests, while some looked quietly pleased.

Jas was sorely tempted to fight back, but not only did she think she wasn't a match for the heavily muscled, highly trained brute, she didn't want to get kicked out of the class. Attacking a member of staff had to be an expelling offence, no matter what the provocation was. The instructor forced her across the room. She felt the bristle of his chin on her neck.

"Think you can take everyone?" he breathed in her ear.

"Kratting Martian scum. Should have stayed where you belong on your filthy colony planet."

He twisted her arm so hard, Jas cried out. She thought he was going to rip her arm from its socket. Once they were at the side of the room where the other students were sitting on the floor to watch the sparring, he relaxed his hold and pushed her down.

There was no space for her. The students shuffled along to get out of the way but they weren't fast enough. The whole thing had taken only a couple of seconds. Jas landed on them, to many exclamations and protests. It was a few moments before everyone could move along and settle into new positions. A couple of friendly students patted her back while Trankle returned to the mat.

Her shoulder hurt badly, and the instructor had humiliated her in front of the rest of the class. She'd done nothing except try her hardest. Wasn't that what they were supposed to do? Tears pricked her eyes and she blinked them away, determined not to let her hurt show.

The hairy student who'd tried to punch her sauntered by on his way back to his spot in the audience. He looked down his nose with a sneer on his face, but Jas noticed with satisfaction that his eye was already turning purple. He would have a shiner by the next day that he'd have to explain somehow. She smiled grimly.

TAMARA WAS SYMPATHETIC. She'd made her chili and rice again. Jas couldn't get enough of it, especially after a long day's training and studying. Tamara loved to cook. She said it relaxed her. She'd gotten into the habit of cooking nearly every day for both of them, diplomatically avoiding all Jas's protests without drawing attention to her lack of creds.

Spooning a heap of chili from a pan onto the rice in Jas's bowl, Tamara said, "What a misborn. I can't believe it. Didn't any of the other students say anything? Are you going to report him?"

"A few of the others stood up for me, but not so loud that he had to take notice." Jas picked up her fork and dug into her meal. She chewed and swallowed a mouthful, then added, shaking her head, "I'm not going to say anything. He didn't leave a mark on me, and neither did that asshole who tried to punch me. It'd be hard to prove I didn't start it."

When Tamara opened her mouth to interrupt, Jas went on, "Believe me, I saw enough of this kind of thing at the children's home. Sure, some of the others might stick up for me and tell the truth about what happened, but some won't. Some'll lie because getting beat by a girl hurt their pride. And who's most likely to be believed? A low-income scholarship student or a member of faculty?"

Jas shrugged. "I don't want to make trouble. I only get one shot at free college. If they throw me out, I won't get another scholarship. I'd have to take out a loan and start over somewhere else next year. I don't know what I'd do for creds between now and then. I'm okay. Don't worry. When you grow up like I did, you get used to this kind of thing."

Tamara pulled out a chair and sat down to eat. "It doesn't seem right to let him get away with it."

"He didn't hurt me that much." Jas sighed. "I don't know why he hates Martians, but he does, and he isn't the first bigot I've met. I don't know why some people hate us. Looking different's a crime to them, I guess. I'll do what I've always done—keep my head down, not attract attention. I'll lose a few fights. That'll take his attention off me."

Tamara tutted and dumped a generous dollop of sour cream onto her food. "Hey, how about we have a party to cheer you up? We can invite some people from the other dorms. From the men's dorms." She raised her eyebrows and grinned.

"Oh, I don't know. It's been kind of a long day." The truth was, Jas wasn't good at parties. It wasn't that she didn't like to make friends, but at parties she always got the feeling that everyone else was following rules she didn't understand. The idea of inviting guys over also didn't appeal that much. Her few forays into the world of romantic relationships—furtive behind the backs of the carers at the children's home—had been awkward and embarrassing. She wasn't good at flirting or anything like that.

"Come on. It'll be fun," Tamara said. "Don't you want to get to know some more people? Or do you want to be a hermit like Aggy? By the way, I heard her arguing with her boyfriend before you came back. Real humdinger it was. Loud enough that I could hear what she was saying through the door. Are you sure you want to spend the evening eavesdropping on her relationship problems?"

Jas groaned and put down her fork. She knew more about Aggy's relationship than she or her boyfriend did. The couple had two settings: blissfully in love or hating each other's guts, and nothing in between. She'd rather fight hairy ass hand to hand again than listen to another episode of the drama that was Aggy's love life. It was also Friday evening and she had no reason to get up early. "Okay, a party it is then."

"Sweet. Let me call some people." Tamara took out her interface and began swiping it with her fingertips while simultaneously forking chili and rice into her mouth with her other hand.

In the space of a month, Tamara seemed to have gotten to know everyone in college. She was constantly receiving messages and disappearing for social engagements. Jas didn't know how she fit it all in along with her studies. Her friend was one of those 'hub' people, effortlessly making connections left, right, and center. She hailed from what remained of New Orleans. Jas wondered if her skills were due to the necessity of making good friends quickly when faced with repeated natural disasters.

Tamara looked up from her screen, her curls bobbing. "All done. People will start arriving about nine. Do you want to give me a hand cleaning the place up? I've ordered drinks and snacks. They should get here in half an hour."

"Sure," Jas replied, wondering if she would navigate this party better than all the others she'd been to. She got up and took the dishes to the compactor. It was nearly full, so she set it to crush and sent the waste down the chute.

She started tidying the kitchen and putting away Tamara's packets of ingredients. In truth, there was little to do. Knowing well the habits of college students, the administration had installed sanobots, which cleaned up the dirt and the debris of everyday life. Jas wasn't sure how they worked, and it had taken her a while to get used to the idea of machines too small to see constantly crawling over every inanimate object in the place. At the children's home, the children had done the cleaning the old-fashioned way.

A loud ping-ping-ping sounded from outside the window. A light was shining in from the midwinter Antarctic darkness. It was the time of year when the sun was little more than a brief glow at the horizon.

Tamara's order had arrived by drone. Jas opened the window and took the boxes from the sling on the underside. She shivered in the downdraft from its four spinning rotors above. As soon as it was empty, the drone sped away into the night, its solitary light quickly lost among the many of McMurdo Sound. Jas put down the boxes and quickly shut the window.

Tamara appeared from her room. She'd changed and tamed her curls into cascading waves. "Thanks," she said when she saw the boxes at Jas's feet. "I'll start setting things out. You go get ready."

"It's okay. I'm not getting changed. I'll help you."

"It's a party, Jas. Don't you want to put a dress on or something?"

"I don't have a dress, and anyway, I'm more comfortable in pants."

"You can't wear the clothes you've been wearing all day. You *must* have something else you can put on. Go and find something." Tamara pointed at Jas's room.

Jas held up her hands. "Okay, okay."

Inside her room, Aggy was fast asleep on her bed, her face streaked with tears. Her most recent fight with her boyfriend had left its mark. Jas didn't doubt that tomorrow Aggy would be back to loudly whispered professions of deepest love.

Jas went to her closet and took out the only remotely fashionable outfit she had. As she was changing, the sound of voices in the living room alerted her to the fact that guests had begun to arrive. She went over to the door and rested her hand on the door knob, hesitating. Maybe now that Aggy was asleep she could have a quiet night in her room? But if she didn't come out, Tamara would notice and come get her. She opened the door and went out.

4

The party had been going for a couple of hours, and things were really warming up. People were drinking and the dancing had started. Jas noticed pills changing hands with little effort at subterfuge. The drugs were certainly hyping up the atmosphere. Illegal drug abuse carried the threat of expulsion, but Jas wasn't much interested anyway. She yawned. She'd chatted with a few people, but she was feeling a little bored and tired.

The music had woken up Aggy about half an hour previously, and she'd appeared from the shared room looking irate and haggard, but her complaints had been ignored. When she gave up, she'd signaled her disapproval by slamming the door.

Tamara was passing through the throng with a plate of snacks. She spotted Jas in the corner and headed over. Dancers' hands reached in to grab the snacks. She had a few left by the time she reached Jas. "Can I interest you in some peanut cheese flakes?"

Jas looked down at the palm-sized crackers. Peanuts and cheese? Was that a Southern thing? "No, thanks. Actually, I'm kinda tired. I might—"

"Aw, you're going to bed so soon? I guessed you might not be enjoying yourself. I thought a party would cheer you up."

"I know, and I appreciate it. I'm just not a—"

A couple had arrived late. Another guest had opened the door to the man and woman. The man was tall with shoulder-length black hair, and the woman he had linked arms with was slim with ashy brown hair cut above her ears. Jas had paused in her conversation with Tamara because something seemed familiar about the man. She peered at him, trying to pin down where it was she'd seen him before.

He was scanning the room while his girlfriend talked to the student who had opened the door. He was idly watching the dancing and chatting party-goers. His gaze found Jas. Their eyes met, and deep inside her, something clicked. The man looked startled.

Even at the distance across the room, Jas saw that his eyes were a deep, rare blue. But it wasn't the color of his eyes that affected her. The sense of recognition she felt was profound. She was also sure that, in fact, she'd never seen him before.

"Jas?" Tamara asked. "Are you okay?"

Jas looked at her friend wordlessly. Tamara turned to find out what she'd been looking at. By then, the blue-eyed man's girlfriend had noticed his preoccupation and was questioning him. She looked annoyed.

"Oh, Sergei and Bree have arrived," said Tamara. "Do you know them?"

"No, I don't think so."

"I'll introduce you. Let's go over."

Panic fluttered in Jas's stomach. "No, it's fine. I think I'll just—"

"It'll only take a minute. You never know, you might have something in common to talk about. Come on. I want you to enjoy yourself." Tamara took Jas's hand and pulled her toward the couple, weaving through the dancers.

Sergei's eyes flicked to Jas again and again as Tamara led her over, though his head was facing his girlfriend.

"Sergei arrived late. He only started college a couple of weeks ago," Tamara shouted as they passed a speaker thumping out bass notes. "He transferred from another college. Someone was saying he *had* to transfer, like it was either that or drop out. Bree didn't waste any time snagging him, and they seem pretty good together. I'm surprised you haven't met him. I thought he was studying security too."

Jas's heart was racing. She also felt sick, but it was a pleasant kind of sickness. She'd never felt that way before. She hoped she would make it through the impending encounter without embarrassing herself.

She and Tamara arrived at the doorway where the couple were still standing. Students were now crushed into the room and it wasn't easy to move. Bree's attention had been diverted by twins in identical party dresses. Sergei was smiling, ready to greet them. Once more, he and Jas locked eyes. She was light-headed.

"Sergei, this is..." Tamara paused as she noticed the look passing between them. "Oh my."

Bree noticed Jas and Tamara and extracted herself from her conversation with the twins. Her hand was still on her boyfriend's arm. She frowned and gave him a little shake, breaking his distraction. "Hi, Tamara. Good to see you again," she said between her teeth.

"Hi Bree," Tamara replied, a little ruefully. "This is Jas. I don't know if you've met."

Sergei held out his hand, and Jas took it. His skin was warm and dry and a little hard, as if he did some kind of manual work. "Hi."

"Hi," Jas replied, feeling like she was greeting an old friend she hadn't seen in a long while.

The five of them started up a conversation about college stuff. It turned out that Sergei was also studying security, but he was taking the domestic option, focusing on anti-theft, including cyber security. Jas was surprised. It was mainly desk work, with maybe some high-level guard duty thrown in. His hands had told her he was more active than that.

Bree was a language specialist studying extraterrestrial communication methods. She hadn't been slow to cotton on to the fact that something was going on between her boyfriend and the tall Martian. Her clear annoyance caused the conversation to sputter to a close, and after an awkward pause, Tamara and Jas withdrew.

They sat down on a sofa behind dancers who were occupying the middle of the room. Jas drew in her long legs to avoid tripping them, while Tamara curled up next to her, tucking her legs beneath herself. She leaned toward Jas's ear to be heard above the music.

"What was *that* about?"

"What?" Jas asked, irritating even herself with her disingenuous reply.

Sergei and Bree were passing through the dancers on their way to the side table that held the snacks and drinks. Every time Sergei's eyes flicked toward her, Jas registered the look inside, like a gong chiming or cymbals clashing.

"Don't play the innocent. You know what I mean," Tamara said. "You and Sergei. I've never seen a look like that before. I didn't believe it ever really happened."

"What do you mean?" Jas replied, tearing her eyes from the black-haired figure looking back at her.

Tamara tutted. "I'm not going to spell it out for you. But are you glad we threw this party now or what?"

"I guess so." Jas smiled sheepishly, though she didn't know what she felt so happy about. Sergei was already with someone, and she hardly had time for her studies, let alone a relationship. What was more, she was planning on flying off to the stars as soon as she graduated. And yet... She glanced up and saw a pair of blue eyes. *Gong. Clash. She'd* never known anything like this either.

5

———————

Jas didn't see Sergei again for a few days. Instead, she spent the weekend witnessing the breakdown of Aggy's long-distance relationship. Her roommate was alternately furious and pleading with her absent boyfriend. Though the woman was irritating as hell, Jas couldn't help but feel sorry for her as she heard her plans for the future slowly unravel.

Jas avoided their shared room as much as possible by studying in the library and going for long walks around town. By Sunday evening, Aggy's many long vidmail conversations finally came to an end, and Jas returned from a walk to find her lying silently on her bed, staring at the blank screen of her interface. "It's over," she said.

Though Jas wasn't sure of the best thing to say or do, she tried to offer some words of friendship and comfort. When that didn't work, she attempted to distract Aggy from her misery by suggesting they do something together. This offer was met with a scornful glance. Aggy cradled her silent interface in her arms like it was a sick baby and turned on her side, presenting Jas with her back.

By the time Jas returned from class on Monday evening, Aggy had gone, for good. Her side of the closet and her desk and shelves were empty. The mattress on her bed was bare. If it hadn't been for her interface in the middle of the floor, its screen shattered, she might never have been there.

Jas sighed with relief and threw herself on her bed. She put her arm over her eyes. With luck, it would be too late in the semester for the college administration to assign another student to the room, and Jas would have it to herself. She would look forward to being alone each morning and night.

There was a tap at the door. Her heart sank. Had Aggy returned? But she had never bothered to knock. Jas called out for her visitor to come in. A black-haired head with blue eyes appeared around the door edge. *Clash. Gong.*

"Hi," Jas tried to say, but her throat had suddenly turned dry. She sat up.

Sergei smiled at her croak. Jas swallowed and tried to look nonchalant.

"I was passing," he said, "and I wanted to say hello. Tamara said you'd just gotten back."

"Oh, yeah, that's right."

"It...er...it turns out we're classmates for a few classes. I just found out you're studying security too. You have a leadership skills class in the morning?"

He'd been asking around about her? "Yes, I do. You're taking that class too?"

"Yeah."

"What's it like?" Sergei asked. "I started late this semester after I transferred from another college. I had to take whatever spare places they had."

"I know. It's good. I mean, the leadership option is good." Jas wondered why she hadn't seen him in class.

Sergei smiled again. "Great. I'll see you tomorrow then." He turned to leave.

"How's..." Jas had only one thing on her mind, but she didn't want to say it. She knew how it would look. But she couldn't help herself. "How's Bree?"

There was that smile again—a knowing smile this time. Sergei was a little cocky. "Oh, we split up. It wasn't really working out."

"I'm sorry."

Sergei's eyebrows lifted. *No, you aren't.*

No, I'm not.

They both laughed a little.

"I'll see you tomorrow," Jas said.

As he closed the door, she lay down and covered her eyes with her arm again. Beneath it, her mouth was curved into a grin.

Sergei sat behind her in the leadership class the next day, which Jas found deeply distracting. She constantly wanted to turn around to look at him, and she felt his gaze on her back like a spot of warm syrup, sweet and tempting. Whenever she did turn around, he was always watching. He would wink at her.

In spite of her pleasant diversion, Jas tried her best to concentrate. In an unpredictable world, her studies had always been the one steady rock she could cling to. She wasn't a natural student—excessive energy made sitting still and paying attention harder for her than most—but her grades were above average, and she planned on keeping them that way.

"In any organization involved in security, there's always a strict hierarchy," the professor was saying. Her name was Clements. "Whether it's one of the armed forces, the police, or a private company's security division, someone at the top gives orders to those directly below them, and so on down the chain to the bottom of the pyramid."

In front of each student was an interface. The screens lit up, and a diagram like a family tree appeared. It was the chain of command in the space navy—a complex list of ranks and related insignia.

Clements continued, "Effectiveness and discipline are built on the foundation of obedience. For the efficient functioning of any group involved in security operations, it's *vital* that each member obeys the commands of those above. They don't have to know why, and sometimes the command might seem odd or even nonsensical. It doesn't matter. In an operating situation, there's no time for discussions, explanations, or justifications. Obedience should be the first response.

"This doesn't only apply to those at the bottom. Compliance is necessary right up the hierarchy.

"Today, we're looking at how a leader's behavior and attitude affects the likelihood of obedience in those below him or her." She picked up a laser pointer.

A hand went up.

Clements glanced at her seating plan. "Mr. Archer?"

The hand's owner, a scruffy young man in a thick jumper, said, "But what if we're told to do something against our conscience? Like, I don't know, kill a kid?"

Clements replied, "Good question. We'll be looking at ethics toward the end of the class, but to give a brief answer, providing the order is lawful, you must obey. However, in the extremely rare event that an order is unlawful, you are legally required to disobey."

Another hand was raised. Before the lecturer had time to check whose it was, a female student said, "How do we tell what's lawful and what isn't? I mean, it isn't like we go through law school."

"Basically it comes down to this," Clements replied, putting down her laser pointer and folding her hands. "If a person of ordinary sense and understanding would judge the order illegal, then you must disobey. To take Mr. Archer's example, it's hard to think of a case where it would be lawful to kill a child. But you must judge each situation according to its context."

The spot of syrup on Jas's back was growing warmer, but she resisted the urge to look around. Something was bothering her about what Clements was saying.

Hers was the third hand to be raised that morning. She waited for Clements to find her name.

"Ms. Harrington?"

"I wanted to ask, what if you're on the ground during a maneuver and you're ordered to do something that doesn't make sense? I mean, what if you think what they're telling you is wrong? If you don't trust their judgment?" She was thinking of Trankle. She'd hate to be serving under him. He'd probably send her on a suicide mission.

Clements snorted a short laugh and replied, "You don't get to make that call about your superiors. Compliance should always be your first response. There's no room for personality clashes in security. It's dangerous. You'll have to accept that you're not going to get along with everyone you work with."

"I understand," Jas replied, "but not everyone we work with is going to be good at their job."

"Ms. Harrington, I know what you mean, but you're muddying the waters here. You have to trust the system that put your superior in his or her position. We can quibble all day about what ifs. As I've been saying for the last five minutes, unquestioning obedience is the bedrock of a successful security operation. From the top down, everyone has to follow orders."

The professor's answer left Jas uncomfortable. Though she hadn't been badly behaved at the children's home, the chaotic nature of the place had left her with a lack of faith in authority. She also wasn't sure she could trust her life to someone like Trankle.

6

After class, Sergei asked Jas if she wanted to come out with him and another few students to a bar in town that Friday evening. She agreed, a little too fast, her stomach fluttering. Anticipation of the casual date made her feel like she was walking through molasses the remainder of the week. Lectures and seminars dragged even more than usual, and in fitness and combat training, she found it hard to concentrate.

It wasn't until Thursday that she saw Sergei again. It turned out that he was also in her weapons class.

They were learning the basics of how the weapons worked, especially the latest powered weapons. It was supposed to improve their skills in handling them. A range of disarmed examples were stored in the classroom: old-fashioned guns, rifles that fired rounds, and the newer 'laser' guns. They were *called* laser guns, but the pulses they emitted were based on the phenomenon of ball lightning. Laser guns emitted short bursts of energy that could shock a living organism's nerves enough to stun it or, when the weapons were set to full power, burn through skin, tissue, and bone.

Firing the laser guns was very different from shooting with bullets. As Jas had discovered during target practice, they didn't produce any recoil, nor any sound apart from a faint fizz. Their range was shorter than projectile weapons', but the strongest wind had no effect on the trajectory. The laser guns were armed with pre-charged power units, and when the energy ran out, they were as useful as an empty pistol.

The students were assigned to groups and given a weapon to take apart and reassemble to understand how it worked. Jas and Sergei were assigned to the same group. As they started, Jas realized where Sergei's firm skin on his hands might have come from. He picked up the laser gun and examined it at eye level, clearly fascinated. He ignored everyone as if he'd forgotten they were there.

On the table was an open case of tiny screwdrivers they'd been given. He ran his fingers through it and took one out. In a few seconds, he carefully removed the casing, revealing a complex system of wires and coils. He bent his head over the weapon, the screwdriver poised in his hand, and closely studied the interior.

Jas folded her arms and looked on, bemused. Another student in the group coughed. Sergei looked up and seemed to remember the others. "Ha, sorry," he said, and pushed the opened weapon to the center of the table where they could see it. He leaned back, and Jas caught his eye. He looked a little embarrassed. "Interesting, huh?"

"Yeah," Jas said, peering into the mysterious inner workings of the gun. "I guess so."

~

IT WAS FINALLY FRIDAY EVENING. Classes were over for the week, and though Jas had a mountain of work to do over the weekend, she could afford to take off the next few hours to relax and enjoy herself. Jas was getting ready to go out. She had to meet Sergei at the front of the college in ten minutes. She'd showered and was trying to decide what to wear. The only clothes she had that were suitable for a bar were the ones she'd worn at the party. She felt a little silly, and poor, to wear the same outfit again. But her height meant that she couldn't borrow anyone else's clothes. Sighing, she began to get dressed.

She was tingling all over in terrified excitement. It seemed inevitable that something would happen with Sergei. Probably something good. She hadn't spent much time examining her feelings for the man—introspection usually led her down roads she didn't want to travel. She couldn't explain what had happened when her eyes had met his in that clichéd way *across a crowded room*. She also couldn't deny the experience, and from his behavior, she didn't think Sergei could either.

Tonight would be interesting to say the least.

She went to Tamara's room. Her friend opened her door at Jas's knock.

"You're going now? You look nice."

It was a white lie, and Jas knew it, but she appreciated it all the same. She'd grown to like Tamara a lot in their short time in the dorm.

"Yeah. You sure you don't want to come?"

"Sorry, you know I'd like to, but I really have too much work to do. We started a whole new section today, on life on high-gravity planets, and I don't know anything about it. We didn't cover the subject at school. I have to go right back to the basics. That's as well as everything else. And we have a test in two weeks."

Tamara's normally cheerful face was looking strained and tired.

"Okay," Jas said. "If you're asleep when I get back, I'll see you in the morning."

"If you get back to your room," Tamara said, and her

dimples appeared.

Jas laughed as a flush crept up her face.

THE NIGHT WAS BITTERLY COLD. Just going from the door of the college to the autocab that awaited her made Jas appreciate the scant warmth of the building's central heating. Two other male students were in the vehicle as well as Sergei. From their behavior toward each other Jas guessed they were a couple. Sergei introduced everyone, and they set off through the brightly lit darkness to the town center.

Alcohol was supposedly banned on campus, but Jas had seen many inebriated students after classes were over for the day. Beer and liquor were easy to purchase in town for those old enough. At eighteen, Jas could legally drink in Antarctica, but she hadn't up to that point. She wasn't against it, she just hadn't sought it out. She supposed tonight would be her first time.

She'd also never been in a bar, she suddenly realized when, after a twenty-minute drive, the cab pulled up outside one in downtown McMurdo Sound. *Rashid's Tavern*, read the sign over the door. It had been cracked and warped by time and the weather. Beneath the wide signage were two windows and a door. The plexiglass windows were divided into small rectangles, separated by lines of brick.

Jas hesitated while the others went directly to the door. Sergei paused, holding the door open and looking back at her. "Something wrong?"

She was wondering why the bar's owner—Rashid—thought it was necessary to have such heavily protected windows. Did they get broken often?

People inside were shouting to Sergei angrily to close the door. "Come on," he said.

Jas hurried inside, faint prickles running up her spine.

7

It was early evening, but the bar was nearly full. Sergei's friends had found a tall table, and they waved them over. All the bar stools were taken, so they stood around the table. Sergei's friend, Aaron, offered to buy the first round. He went over to the bar and attracted the bartender's attention. As the woman turned around, Jas was startled by her face.

The bartender had either had extensive surgery or she wasn't human. Her skin was patterned yellow and brown, and where her mouth and nose should have been was a prehensile snout with whiskers on either side. She nodded as she took Aaron's order. When she moved down the bar to make the drinks, he turned back to them with raised eyebrows, as if to say, *Did you see?*

"Is that Rashid, do you think?" Jas asked Sergei.

"Rashid? Who's Rashid?"

"The bar owner," Jas replied. "Didn't you see the sign? It said Rashid's Tavern."

"Did it? Krat. The autocab's brought us to the wrong place. Terry, you told it where to go. What did you say?"

"I gave it the address you told me."

"I don't think you did," Sergei said. "Maybe you misheard me. Come to think of it, this doesn't look much like a student bar."

Jas had been wondering about that too. While waiting for Aaron to bring their drinks, she'd been looking around at the crowd. They definitely weren't students. They were older, and they didn't look the types to be interested in education. Their faces were roughened and red from cold exposure, and they wore clothes representing fashions of several decades, including many items that were timeless, such as thick, shapeless coats and hats. Judging by the behavior of some, they'd been drinking for several hours already.

No one dressed up to go out to this bar.

As Jas was looking, a man turned to meet her gaze. Gray-blond stubble coated his chin and cheeks and grew not much longer on his head. A tattoo of an anarchist symbol ran up the side of his face. The man leered as he looked Jas in the eyes, revealing weirdly decorated perfectly square teeth. She turned away uneasily.

"Checking out the local action?" Sergei asked.

She laughed. "No."

"Sure you don't see anyone you like?" His face was mock serious.

Jas took another look around the room at the crowd of locals. She was beginning to understand McMurdo Sound. It was where people came when they wanted to escape something, whether it was the law, a relationship, family, or social conventions. Her spine was still tingling strangely.

"Do you think maybe we should go somewhere else?" she asked Sergei.

Aaron arrived, his large hands wrapped around four glasses of beer that he deposited on the table. Sergei passed them around, picked up his own and took a sip. "Do you really want to leave? It's cold outside, and it's going to be hard to get a cab now that the evening rush is on. Let's stay here a while. Seems friendly enough."

Aaron asked, "Did you get a look at the bartender? Where do you think she's from?"

"How would we know?" Terry asked. "She could be from anywhere."

"I mean what planet," Aaron replied. "She isn't human. Couldn't you tell from her face?"

"She could easily be human. Doesn't matter what she looks like," said Terry. "You can get all kinds of things done these days. Between surgery and gene therapy, you can look like a woolly mammoth if you want."

"No," replied Aaron, "she's definitely alien—if she is a she. Did you get a look at her hands? I'm using the word loosely."

As Aaron and Terry continued their discussion about the origins of the bartender, Sergei moved a little closer to Jas. If he'd been anyone else, he would have been a little too close for her preferences, but she found herself welcoming the proximity.

She sipped her beer. It tasted bitter but not unpleasant. She wondered when she would start to feel the effects of the alcohol. "You like weapons, then?" she asked Sergei, raising her voice to compete with the increasing hum of conversation in the bar.

"What makes you think that?"

"You seemed very interested the other day in class."

"Oh, right. I guess I was, but not because it was a weapon. I like taking things apart to find out how they work. That's all." He undid his coat. The place was getting warmer. "So you're in the deep space program?"

"Yes."

He shook his head slightly. "Doesn't the idea of starjumping freak you out? But you must have already made at least one jump from Mars."

"I did, but just the one. It was okay." She tensed, wondering if Sergei would move the conversation on to her background, but he didn't.

"Doesn't it scare you just a little bit?" he asked. "I mean, I don't think they even know exactly how starjumps work, do they?"

"Hmm...from what I understand, they know the math, they just don't know where the starship actually goes while it's in a jump state."

"Huh, I'd like to see other planets, but I don't know that I could make the trip, you know?"

"I guess I know what you mean, but it is a tested technology. People are starjumping all over the galaxy these days. Maybe if you could take apart a starship engine and look inside?"

Sergei laughed. "Maybe." He took a swig of beer.

More people were arriving, blasts of icy wind accompanying them whenever the door to the bar opened. Music started playing from speakers, and Sergei and Jas had to draw even closer together to hear each other speak. They talked about their classes and professors, life at college, and other students.

Jas found herself suddenly telling Sergei about her background. She told him about her first memories of life in the Valles Marineris Institute for Cared-For Children—how one day she'd asked why other children lived with their parents, and how the care worker had told her abruptly that both her parents had died years ago. She also told him about the bureaucratic hiccup that had resulted in her being sent to Earth almost too late for her body to adapt to the higher gravity. She even told him of the difficulty of life at the new children's home, and how she'd been bullied over her height and origins.

Sergei listened gravely as Jas's story poured out. She didn't know why she was telling him about her life, except that it felt right. He didn't comment much, seemingly sensing her need to just get it all out, and she was grateful for that. As her story wound down and finished at the time she left for college, he put his hand on her shoulder. He was looking at her so intently, she wondered if he was about to kiss her.

To break the tension, she asked, "How about you? How did you end up here?"

Sergei put down his glass. "Well, I can't compete with you in the interesting childhood stakes."

As he went to speak, Aaron folded his arms and leaned on the opposite side of the table, causing it to rock. Their glasses fell over, and beer splashed everywhere.

"Krat," Sergei exclaimed.

A woman standing with her back to them turned round as beer splashed down her legs. "What the hell?" she said. She was with a man, and they were both locals, judging from their weather-beaten looks and oddly cut hair. The man peered over to see what had happened. A sly look passed between him and the woman.

"Hey, you're gonna pay to get her pants cleaned," he growled.

"What?" Terry said. "It's only beer. It'll wash out."

"You think I wash my clothes myself?" the woman asked. "Who the hell does that these days? I pay for all my cleaning, and these are genuine imitation sealskin. They cost me a fortune."

"Look, man," said Aaron, "I'm sorry, but we're students. We're not rolling in creds." Aaron's words only caused the man and woman to scowl more deeply. "I didn't mean to mess up your pants. How about if I wipe them down with something wet? That should get most of it off. It isn't like this beer's strong."

The man and woman were clearly taking advantage and trying to scam Aaron out of some money. But it was going to be hard to avoid giving them something. The man grabbed the front of Aaron's coat.

"Get his credchip, Marl. I got a reader here somewhere." She felt inside large pockets in her jacket.

Sergei gripped Marl's arm. "Let go of my friend."

"Hey," Jas said, raising her hands. "It's okay. I'll pay. Look, here's my chip." She held out her wrist.

Around them, the chatter in the bar quietened. The bar's patrons had noticed the dispute and were watching. The bartender was on an interface talking to someone.

"No, Jas. Don't pay them a cred," Sergei said. "It's only a little beer. They're out of line."

Aaron looked down disbelievingly at the hand grasping his coat.

Marl shifted his gaze from Aaron's face to Sergei's hand on his arm. Jas knew what was about to happen, even if Sergei was oblivious. He had less than a second. She could either say something to try to cool the situation, or stop Marl from punching him. She didn't have time for both. She made her decision.

As Marl released his grip on Aaron, she picked up one of the fallen beer glasses. As he drew back his fist, she got ready to throw. Marl's punch was about to land on Sergei's surprised face when the glass hit Marl on his forehead. It didn't stop the blow from falling, but it lessened its impact.

Sergei fell back, and Marl's attention was diverted to a new enemy—Jas. His lip lifted in a snarl. But the students had worse problems. At that bar for locals, when it came to a dispute, there could be no doubt about whose side the patrons would take. They began to murmur angrily. Terry had realized the danger of their situation too. "Let's go," he shouted, and began pulling Aaron toward the door.

A punch landed on the back of Jas's head, and the table loomed up as she fell forward. She caught herself before she hit it and turned dizzily to face her attacker, but all she could see was Sergei's back as he jumped on her assailant.

It was a fight they could never win, and if they didn't get out soon, they might never get out. Jas grabbed Sergei and pulled him off the man who had punched her. Blows and kicks began to rain down on both of them. Aaron and Terry seemed to have made some progress toward the door, and holding Sergei back as best she could, Jas edged over in their direction.

A particularly hard kick landed on her right shin, and she cried out. Sergei had calmed down a little, but he became inflamed again and struck out at a local. "Stop it," Jas yelled. "We've got to get out."

Somehow, they all managed to make it to the door and out into the street. As soon as they were outside, they ran. Jas and Sergei went one way, Aaron and Terry another. A few streets away, Jas and Sergei drew to a halt. The locals had given up their pursuit.

Sergei began to laugh. Jas couldn't understand why.

"What's so funny?" she asked. "We could have been killed back there. We were lucky to get away."

He controlled his guffaws. "You're right. I'm sorry. It was kind of fun, though, wasn't it? How's your head?"

Jas recalled the punch and put her hand to the back of her scalp. A painful lump was forming. "I'm okay. How's your eye?"

Sergei touched his face where Marl had punched him. "I don't know. Can you take a look?"

Jas went over and brought her face close to his to assess the damage in the dim streetlight. It was only when she was centimeters from him that she realized his ploy. He was gazing into her eyes. It was her turn to chuckle, a little nervously. She drew back. A silence stretched out, thin and tight as a drum skin.

Tension knotted Jas's stomach. "It's weird, isn't it? This...feeling we have." Had she just made a fool of herself?

She'd thought he was experiencing the same strange attraction as she was. What if he wasn't? Had she misinterpreted the looks that had passed between them? Was she just another girl to him?

"It is weird," Sergei said. "When I saw you at Tamara's party, it was like..." He paused. "It was like I'd known you all my life, only I hadn't met you, until then." His eyes were black in the darkness.

Jas nodded. Neither said anything. They had stopped in a short alleyway, where the illumination from the street lights barely reached. The winter cold was biting Jas's face. She wondered what would happen next.

Was this how it was for other people? From what she'd seen of romantic relationships, she didn't think so. On the other hand, friends had told her about meeting *the one*. Was there something she was supposed to say? *Was* there anything to say? As with many things, there seemed to be rules to the situation that she didn't understand.

Sergei touched her upper arm and stepped closer.

Jas said, "Is this the part where we—"

He kissed her.

8

───────

The buzz about the bar fight between students and locals—which apparently had been started by a female student throwing a beer glass—died down after a while. The bar didn't have cameras trained on its patrons, so no one could prove who had been the instigator, though verbal descriptions pointed fingers strongly at the only Martian on campus.

Jas's combat training instructor didn't need anything like firm evidence to support his opinion on the subject. His prejudice against her increased to the extent that he virtually ignored her in class and routinely 'forgot' to include her in sparring sessions. This was doubly annoying to her: combat skills would be essential in her job, and hand-to-hand fighting was about the only thing that she naturally learned quickly. Everything else she had to work for.

Meanwhile, all the other students except for Tamara had started to keep their distance. People she thought had been her friends began to pretend they didn't see her in the corridors between classes. If Tamara and Sergei were busy, she ate lunch alone in the cafeteria. She seemed to have gained the reputation of being aggressive from the combat class too, which didn't help.

Jas didn't know what to do about it, or even if she should do something. Maybe she didn't need friends who believed in gossip rather than finding out the truth from her. Tamara told her that she put straight anyone who talked about Jas within her earshot, but everyone knew they were friends and probably concluded that Tamara's judgment was clouded. Jas didn't think there was any point in defending herself. Anything she said would seem like an excuse or justification.

Her growing relationship with Sergei was the saving grace of the whole situation. As far as she could without slipping too far behind with her work, she spent every spare moment with him. After a couple of blissful weeks of having her room to themselves, another late transfer arrived and was allocated the empty place.

Sergei also shared, so they couldn't be alone in his room without inconveniencing his roomie. He solved the problem by persuading Aaron to help him build something vaguely resembling an igloo a little way out of town. It was a chilly setting for love trysts, and they couldn't run a heater too long without the walls melting and ice-water pooling on the floor, but Jas didn't care. Wherever they were, being with him was enough, and he seemed to feel the same about her.

Yet Jas wasn't so blindly in love that she couldn't see they were very different. Sergei didn't work as hard or pay as much attention to his studies as she did. He wasn't the stereotypical 'bad boy', but he didn't care about his grades, or even if he would make it to graduation. He often missed class because he was working on something in his room. In fact, one of advantage of the igloo was that wires, transistors, silicon ships and other paraphernalia weren't strewn around the place. In the igloo, Jas didn't suddenly become aware that a part from a motherboard was sticking in her back.

Sergei avoided Jas's hints at questions about why he'd transferred from his previous college, but she had a strong suspicion it had something to do with flunking out. She didn't press him for an answer. She didn't really care. He was a good, kind person, and he didn't have any addictions or vices, unless he hid them very well.

The only thing that niggled her was the fact that, if they both continued along their current paths, it would be hard for them to be together. She was studying to work in security on a starship, he was studying to...well, Sergei had no particular ambition, if the truth was told, but whatever it was that he did, it would never be aboard a starship with Jas. He had a deep dislike of the idea of traveling in space. Airplanes, he could handle, he'd said. Maybe even shuttles, though given the choice he'd rather not travel by them, but he seemed to have an actual phobia of deep space travel. The idea of disappearing from the physical universe, even for the few seconds that most starjumps took, sent chills down his spine.

It wouldn't be fair for Jas to expect Sergei to wait the months or years a mission took, only to see her for a few weeks before she left again. As Jas could find no solution to this problem, she pushed it to the back of her mind and concentrated on enjoying the time that they had together. Decisions about their long-term future could wait. Maybe she would be content with an Earth-based job.

JAS WAS a little late for her zero-g combat training class, and when she arrived, she was surprised to find no one had changed into their swimwear. Though starship gravity drives could create gravitational forces, no one had invented a machine that could turn gravity off. The usual training for zero-g fighting consisted of underwater training. The students used rebreathers and practiced by using the swimming pool walls and each other as solid surfaces from which to propel themselves. No actual swimming was allowed as in space or a gaseous atmosphere that wouldn't work.

The instructor—a man called Elba—had explained that water wasn't much of a substitute for no gravity, but it was the best they could do for regular training sessions.

Jas bypassed the changing rooms and went to the only remaining seats, which were at the top of the tiered benches that bordered the swimming pool. As she sat down, she realized the instructor was going over their scheduled real zero-g training exercise in space. Her shoulders sagged. The training trip was taking place over the next weekend, and all she knew about it was that it cost a lot—far more than she could afford. She hoped it didn't count as a large percentage of their final grade.

"And I have a little surprise for you all," said the instructor. "Normally, this class would visit an orbiting space station for this training weekend. We'd be training in micro-gravity rather than zero-g, in fact. But I have a friend who runs an interplanetary import/export company, and it just so happens that this weekend she has a special consignment she has to take to Mars."

Elba paused for effect, scanning the students' faces. "She's agreed to let us all travel on her ship at a discounted price that matches the usual fee. We'll complete a starjump and train in real zero-g for a whole day."

The students hollered and clapped, except for Jas. A trip to Mars would have been nice. The thought of returning for a visit there crossed her mind fairly often. Still, she thought, she would have a whole weekend with Sergei.

Elba went over the details of the trip and what the students had to bring with them. Then he took questions. He spent the remainder of the class explaining the combat techniques they would be practicing, and what differences the students could expect when sparring in zero-g.

Class finished a little early. Jas put her bag over her shoulder, ready to leave. She had to wait for most of the students to file out before she could make her way down the stairs between the benches. As she went past Elba, he stopped her. "Could I speak to you for a moment, Ms. Harrington?"

He waited until the last student had departed, then said, "Can I ask, is something wrong? You looked a little down in class today. Aren't you excited about our trip?"

"It does sound exciting, and I hope you all have a great time, but I can't come."

"Is there a problem? Do you have something planned for the weekend? If so, I'm afraid it'll have to wait. The real-life zero-g training isn't optional. It counts toward your final assessment."

"Yeah, I thought it might." Jas sighed. "You see, I'm a scholarship student. I don't have the creds to—"

"Is that all? Then there's no problem. Jas, you need to read your entitlements document properly. Any mandatory class materials, equipment, and other expenses—including class trips—are covered by your scholarship. It would be a little silly if they weren't, wouldn't it? What's the point of awarding a scholarship if the student can't complete a whole class and graduate?"

"It's all paid for?"

"Everything's covered. *Everything.* You don't have to worry about it."

"You mean, I get a trip to Mars for free?"

The man's face fell a little. "I'm sorry, but we won't be landing on Mars. There isn't time, and if there were, Mars has far too many visitation controls. We wouldn't be able to arrange visas and health checks. But you will get to experience a starjump and real zero-g. That's something, isn't it?"

A tiny flicker of hope that had flared up in Jas sputtered out. She'd gone from expecting to miss out on a trip, to anticipating a visit to her birth planet, and then to the lesser delight of a space trip, within less than a minute.

"Yeah, it is something," she said.

9

Jas was with Sergei. They were on the sofa in her dorm living room, and Tamara was in the kitchen cooking dinner. Jas was leaning on her boyfriend, resting her head on his shoulder and stretching an arm around his waist. He was wearing a thick sweater that felt soft and comfortable against her face. His arm was draped over her shoulders.

Sergei was telling her about something broken that he'd been trying to repair. Jas had forgotten what it was he was talking about. She was content to listen to the sound of his voice and feel the slight vibration of his throat and chest as he spoke.

She'd spent the afternoon doing her fitness training, first on the all-weather track and then on the machines in the fitness center. Her muscles ached pleasantly. She wondered if Sergei would give her a massage later. Slowly, her eyes began to close.

A kiss on the top of her head woke her up.

"Am I that boring to listen to?" Sergei asked. "You were snoring."

Jas sat up. "Sorry. But you fixed it, right?"

"Yeah, I fixed it." He smiled and held out his arm, inviting her to snuggle up again.

Jas returned to her position, but immediately sat up again. "Hey," she said. "I just remembered. We had weapons today. You skipped class."

"Yeah, I had to—"

"Again."

"Yeah, but—"

"You're going to fail if you don't attend. You'll get kicked out of school. Then how will we be together?"

"Don't worry," Sergei replied, pulling her in for a kiss. "I'll get a job as a custodian."

There was a cough. Tamara had appeared from the kitchen carrying two plates. She put them down as Jas and Sergei drew apart. She'd made avocado-boat starters. Jas wondered where she'd found avocados in Antarctica.

Tamara sat down in an armchair across from the sofa. She rested her elbows on her knees and her chin in her hands as she gazed at the couple. "You two are so cute." She sighed. "Come on. Eat up. The main course is almost ready." She returned to the kitchen.

Jas passed Sergei a plate. "I'm leaving early tomorrow for the spaceport."

"Huh? Oh, I forgot. Your Mars trip. That's tomorrow, is it? How long will you be gone for?"

"Only two days."

"Two days to Mars and back. How long did the first mission take? Two years?"

"Something like that." Jas wondered how long it had taken to get to Mars when her parents emigrated there. Had they been among the original settlers, or had they been part of the global warming rush? She'd been born on Valles Mariniers Five, scene of the worst colony disaster in the history of humankind's expansion into space. A massive explosion—

possibly originating in the oxygen storage tanks—had devastated the base. Only those at the periphery had survived the initial blast, and then only for the few seconds it took the fireball to reach them.

Jas had never researched the disaster. A care worker at the children's home on Mars had once offered to show her the records of the couples of fertile age who had died, but she hadn't wanted to speculate about which of the twenty or so might have been her parents. She'd never been able to see the point.

"Are you sure you'll be okay doing this starjump, Jas?" Sergei asked. "Is your instructor's friend legit? Is her ship safe?"

She put down her fork and touched the side of his face. His concern was heart-warming, though she knew it was also borne out of his distrust of space travel. "I'll be fine. In fact, though I'll miss you, I'm looking forward to it. Don't worry. I'll be back before you know it."

THE *ALEXANDRIA IV* WAS A MID-RANGE, multi-purpose utility vessel of the type often purchased by space entrepreneurs who were just starting out. The ship's design didn't define a specific business strategy, allowing the flexibility to alter direction if the first venture didn't work out. It had a hold generous enough for a substantial shipment, the crew's quarters, and twenty modest passenger berths.

It was also a ship for spacefarers who never settled on one thing. They spent their lives roaming the stars, picking up a group of colonists here, a shipment there, taking whatever work they could find wherever they could find it, eking out a living.

Jas could see the appeal of such a life, she thought as she arrived by shuttle from the McMurdo Sound Spaceport. The white-streaked, brilliant blue globe that was Earth slowly rotated to one side, and through the shuttle windows on the other side of the passenger cabin, she could see the *Alexandria IV*, its long snout taking up the view. The snout was mostly engine, that much Jas knew. The technology that enabled star-jumps was bulky. Aside from that, she wasn't sure what they would find inside.

After docking with the other vessel, the students filed through the opening that linked the shuttle and the starship, Elba bringing up the rear. A small, wiry woman met them in the narrow, bare-metal corridor. She greeted them and Elba when she appeared, and directed the students to follow her, explaining the layout of the ship as they went.

Jas was immediately taken back to the first and only star-jump she'd ever experienced, when traveling to Earth at the age of twelve. She'd been alone and lonely. Her Martian friends had either already left for Earth a year or two before her, or they'd still been too young to make the trip. Aside from that, she couldn't remember much of what had happened.

"Here are your cabins," the ship's owner announced they drew close to a set of ten doors, five on each side of the corridor. "You can figure out which ones you're taking later—they're all doubles, so you'll have to share. Before you enter your cabins, I'm going to take you to the jump suite. You need to know where you'll have to be in around four hours, when we've maneuvered far enough away from Earth and built up energy for the jump. Please make sure you aren't tardy. Time's money."

"Don't worry," said Elba. "They won't be late." He was in the lead now, walking alongside his friend, and he shot a look over his shoulder to impress the instruction on his students.

The jump suite was only just large enough for the twenty-five jumpseats it held. The smell of the foam and plastic reclined seats made Jas a little nauseous. Open safety harnesses hung down from them. Memories of her first jump returned to

Jas at the sight. She recalled the crew members finding her a spare adult seat as the child-sized one had been too small.

"Isn't there a window?" one of Jas's male classmates asked. "I wanted to look outside as we jumped."

"No windows on starships, son, and you wouldn't see anything if there were," replied the owner. "You'd only notice the stars had changed position."

"So it really is like falling asleep and waking up?" another student asked.

"Hmm..." said the woman, "it's more like falling down a well, then being suddenly thrust to the surface again. You'll float for thirty seconds or so as the gravity comes back online. There are sick bags in the slots on your seats. If anyone feels like they're going to throw up, hold the bag around your mouth, okay? I'm sure you can all imagine what it's like when someone upchucks in zero-g. If you can't, I don't want you finding out aboard my ship. I take it you can all remember the way here from the cabins? We jump at eleven hundred sharp. Meanwhile, you can make use of the passenger lounge and the cafeteria, but you're not to enter any crew areas. They're clearly signed."

"Are we doing the training when we arrive?" the male classmate asked Elba.

"No. We'll be training in the cargo bay, so we'll have to wait for the Mars shuttle to collect the shipment. Then we'll move out of orbit and turn off the gravity for a few hours."

At eleven hundred, Jas was strapped into a jumpseat, listening to the countdown. The ship's owner had explained that the seats weren't to protect them from violent movements of the ship, but from any accidents that might occur.

Jas briefly wondered what kind of accidents were possible, but there was no time to ask. Maybe Sergei was right about space travel. The trip seemed like a lot of work for just a few hours' training, and she wouldn't even be able to go to Mars.

The owner, Elba and three crew members with the coloring and build of Martians were also strapped into jumpseats. A vibration began building all around them. It was in Jas's seat and in the air. The jump suite walls also seemed to subtly shaking. The movement penetrated her skin, her teeth, and her bones. Over the speaker came the sound of the pilot's voice, counting *four, three, two, one, zero.*

Then Jas fell.

10

It was hard to believe that, after several hours of building energy, the engines released it all in a split second and catapulted the *Alexandria IV* tens of millions of kilometers across the solar system. Was catapulted the right word? It was more like the ship and everyone and everything in it had disappeared out of existence for a millisecond, only to reappear in an entirely different place. Jas had a sense of climbing or clawing her way back to the physical universe—to life.

The experience had left her more shaken than she'd thought it would. She didn't recall feeling so disoriented the first time around. She wasn't the only one affected. A couple of students had made use of the sick bags. After the artificial gravity had started up, everyone but the owner and crew crowded into the cafeteria for a warm drink to settle their stomachs.

Jas was squashed between the petite classmate that she was sharing a cabin with and the male student who had been asking the questions about starjumps. No one was saying much. As Jas recovered a little, she decided that starjumping wasn't too bad, and she wouldn't mind doing it more regularly.

A woman in a flightsuit came in. Her eyes searched the students crowded at the tables, and when she saw Jas, she beckoned her with a finger. The others watched as Jas got up and made her way over to the woman. She had to be the pilot as she hadn't been in the jump suite during the jump. She lacked the Martian coloring of the other crew members, so Jas assumed she was from Earth. She followed the woman out of the cafeteria and into the corridor.

"They said we had a Martian student aboard," the pilot remarked when they were out of earshot of the other students.

"I guess I'm not difficult to spot."

"Do you get back to Mars often?"

"No, I haven't been since I was twelve."

The pilot nodded, though Jas had a suspicion that the woman was asking questions she already knew the answers to, out of politeness. Jas's scholarship student background was hardly a secret.

"We don't often have passengers, you know," the pilot went on as Jas accompanied her, wondering where they were going. "Owens usually runs shipments. The regular transports get most of the passenger traffic. She can't compete on price."

"Oh," Jas said.

"And when we do have passengers, it's usually a bad idea to invite them to the flight deck. You never know when someone's going to accidentally flip a switch or touch a screen."

"You're taking me to the flight deck?" Jas asked.

"Of course, where did you think we were going?"

"I didn't know."

"Here we are," the pilot said. She put the flat of her hand to a panel, and a door slid open.

Jas could see another good reason for not inviting passengers to that part of the ship: the place was tiny. Two seats took up nearly all the available floor space. In front of and above the seats were interface screens, switches, and buttons. That was it.

That was all there was room for. Jas wasn't even sure how the pilot got into her seat.

She still didn't know why she was there.

"Can you squeeze in okay?" the pilot asked her as she made a deft maneuver that somehow landed her in her seat. Jas's movements were far less graceful as she clambered and twisted her way into a sitting position, almost elbowing the pilot in the head. Apparently, she was about to get a lesson in flying a starship, though she had no idea why.

The pilot reached forward, but stopped midway to a screen and turned to Jas. "You do know why I've brought you here, don't you?"

"Umm...not exactly."

The pilot laughed. "Sorry for not explaining. I thought it was obvious. You'd like to see Mars, right? It's okay if you'd rather not."

"No, I'd love to," Jas replied, realizing the truth of the words as they left her mouth. She did want to see her home planet, desperately. "But I thought there were no windows on starships?"

"There aren't, but pilots can get a visual if we need one." She held a finger over the largest interface, directly in front of both seats. "Ready?"

Jas gripped her arm rests. She nodded.

The pilot swiped the screen, and an image of a red planet appeared. The *Alexandria IV* was in orbit. The curved, deep red Martian surface spread from horizon to horizon below them. The pilot explained how they'd arrived from their starjump some distance away, then navigated into orbit to await the cargo shuttle's arrival, but Jas only barely took in her words. The image of Mars was sinking into her mind.

"Where's Valles Marineris? Can we see it from here?" she blurted.

"Is that where you grew up? It's on the other side of the

planet at the moment. It should be coming around in half an hour or so, if you want to wait."

"Yes, yes, I do." Jas rested her elbows just below the screen, taking care to avoid touching anything else. She scanned the rust-red image, and as she looked more closely, she began to notice patches of dark red and gray that had to be the settlements. They were set in squares, rectangles, and spreading starbursts.

She remembered the blue-green, cloud-swirled surface of Earth she'd seen from the shuttle windows. Mars was dry and barren, and it didn't resemble anything like her memory of it. She recalled the camaraderie and warmth of the children's home among her friends. Though they were all orphaned or abandoned or removed from their parents due to abuse, they'd found a kind of family with each other. Dysfunctional and sometimes unpredictable to be sure, but a family nonetheless. The image she saw before her seemed hardly capable of supporting the pulsing life and energy of humanity.

After a little while, the pilot pointed out that Valles Marineris was coming into view. To Jas's eye, it looked the same as the rest of the surface. She could hardly believe those lines that ran out from the valley bottom and up the sides of the surrounding mountains were once the scene of the disaster that had claimed her parents' lives, or that she had once been a tiny baby there. Had it been her mother or her father who had put her in the safety capsule? Why hadn't they gotten in with her? She wished she could meet them and tell them she'd made it.

A keen yearning grew in her heart. She wanted to travel to new planets. For years, she'd entertained the idea of a career in deep space as a possibility—something interesting and challenging to do with her life. But seeing that dusty expanse of alien soil slowly revolving beneath the ship had turned her idea into much more than that. Space travel wasn't something she was choosing to do, it was something she *had* to do.

Her heart sank. Space travel also meant a life without Sergei. He would never come with her.

"What do you think of Mars?" asked the pilot.

Jas sighed. "I think I've seen enough. Thanks."

She awkwardly climbed out of her seat and left to go to her cabin.

The room was empty. Her classmate was probably in the cafeteria with the others. Jas lay down on the bottom bunk, curled on her side. She wondered what she was going to say to Sergei when she got back to campus.

11

———

The cloud of her decision hung over Jas throughout the Mars trip, and when she got back to McMurdo Sound, Sergei could tell immediately that something was wrong. She didn't waste any time in telling him. It wasn't fair to allow things to continue as they were when the relationship had no future.

Jas didn't cry easily, but the tears were soon pouring down her face as she explained what she'd realized when she'd seen Mars. She felt like she was being torn in two. She didn't think she'd ever love someone again like she loved this man, but neither could she be happy Earth-bound.

As Jas went on, Sergei looked down and swallowed. Her explanation drew to a close, and he looked up with a forced smile. "It's okay. I'll just learn to like space travel."

She put a hand to his face. "No, you won't."

He shrugged. "People change. Maybe you won't feel the same way in a couple of years. Maybe I'll get over my fear. I could try hypnosis. Or drugs."

They laughed, sadly.

"No drugs," Jas said.

"But we'll stay together for now?"

Jas nodded and wiped her eyes. "For now."

Jas's studies continued, and soon it was time for her weekly hand-to-hand combat session with Trankle. Jas had avoided confrontation with him as much as she could, especially since the bar incident. Whenever he criticized her for a mistake she hadn't made, or when he passed over her when picking students for sparring, she gritted her teeth and let it go.

The session had started out like the rest. She'd stayed at the back and avoided the man's gaze. But it wasn't enough. Maybe her depression over a future without Sergei was showing on her face, or maybe Trankle took her morose expression personally. During his explanation that the class was to be about techniques for defeating a larger opponent, he stopped twice to stare at her. The other students also looked at her curiously, as if to figure out what was bothering the instructor.

"Don't be intimidated by size," Trankle said after his second pause. He addressed all the students but then fixed Jas with a glare. "It doesn't matter how big the other guy or girl is, you've got advantages. Speed, agility, and—if you've learned anything in this class—technique. If you have time, play the long game. Wear your opponent out. Some heavier types slack off on their cardio-vascular. Got no stamina. It goes without saying, but avoid grappling. Duck in, and hit the vulnerable spots, hard. Throat, diaphragm, solar plexus, groin, kidneys. If your opponent doesn't go down on your first attack, back up and wait for the next opening."

He paused again and threw Jas another look.

"Harrington," he barked. "What's your problem?"

Jas was startled. "What?" She'd been following what he was saying. Not closely, but she'd been listening.

"Think you know better, huh? Get over here."

The students shuffled aside as Jas made her way to the front. Tension rose in the room. All the students knew Trankle's antipathy toward Jas. The atmosphere became tense.

"There." The instructor pointed at the mat. Jas went over and stood where he'd pointed, her muscles tensing. An uncomfortable prickling began running up and down her spine.

"These techniques are useful for women fighting men," Trankle went on. "Ninety-nine times out of a hundred, the guy's gonna be bigger and stronger. But with the right moves, a woman *can* incapacitate a man. Harrington here's the biggest woman among you. By far," he added. A few of the students snickered, though many looked grave and embarrassed. "If any girl among you stands a chance of taking me out, it's her. Wanna try it, Harrington? I'm guessing you do."

He joined her on the mat and got ready to fight, bending and spreading his arms and legs. He fixed his narrow eyes on her, as if to say, *Now's your chance, bitch.*

Jas's arms hung limply at her sides. The whole situation was ridiculous. The teaching method Trankle had used up until then was to first demonstrate a technique, then ask the students to practice it. Now, he was expecting her to practice techniques that he hadn't taught.

Jas debated pointing this out, but Trankle's lips were thin, and his bull neck was taut. He looked really mad. He was only going to get madder if she questioned his methodology in front of the other students. She would have to do as he said and try to fight him.

She was thankful for the protective sparring gear she was wearing. A head and face guard and body shield were the only advantages she had over this burly, expert fighter. He didn't deign to put on the safety gear that the students had to wear.

Jas began to circle the mat, and Trankle turned to follow her. "Not bad, Harrington. So you *did* think you had something to learn from this class." He lunged and grabbed, but Jas hopped backward, out of his reach. She quickly sidestepped to the other side of the mat. Trankle spun around and lunged again, but Jas repeated the same avoidance maneuver.

"Gonna try and tire me out, huh?" said Trankle "Sad for you, we don't have time for that." He stopped moving and straightened up. Beckoning with his fingertips, he said, "Attack me."

Jas was also still. She looked into Trankle's hate-filled eyes. The watching students were silent and unmoving, seemingly holding a collective breath.

"C'mon," the instructor said. "What are you scared of? You're wearing your safety gear. I can't hurt you." He moved his hands from his head to his hips. "Look at me. Get a lucky hit, and you could do me a lot of damage. C'mon, Harrington. I know you want to."

Still Jas hung back. What did he want from her? To beat her. That was what he wanted. He wanted to defeat her, to hurt the filthy Martian. He knew she'd been pulling punches and throwing her matches. He wanted to show her she had something to be scared of.

Her gaze flicked to the watching students. Some were looking on sympathetically. Did they realize Trankle's intentions too? But there was nothing any of them could do to help. They had to obey him as much as she did.

"Harrington," the instructor barked, making Jas jump. "I gave you an order. Or do you only fight people weaker than you?"

Anger flared up in Jas, and without thinking, she rushed in and kicked upward, trying to reach the man's head. He deftly caught her ankle one-handed. Grabbing her foot with the other hand, he twisted her leg cruelly around. Jas's body followed. She cried out in pain, and suddenly she was face downward on the mat, her knee and hip agonized.

The students gasped.

Jas was still, waiting for the pain in her leg to dissipate. Her face smarted where it had slid along the mat.

"Get up, Harrington," Trankle said. "Quit faking. I didn't hurt you that bad."

Wincing, Jas stood up, wobbling. She limped to the back of the audience, the students parting silently to let her through.

"Harrington provided us with a great example of what *not* to do," said Trankle. "Now we're gonna look at some *effective* ways you can beat a stronger opponent."

"Wow, tough class today?" Sergei asked when he met Jas for dinner in the cafeteria that evening. He was referring to the bright red abrasion on Jas's face from its encounter with the training mat. He put down his tray and sat opposite her.

"Tough instructor," Jas replied and went on to explain what had happened.

"What an asshole," Sergei exclaimed. "Did you report him?"

"No point," Jas said. "I can't prove he was doing anything other than a normal training exercise."

"Jas, you can't let him treat you like that. Some of the other students will back you up. They saw what happened."

Jas sighed. "It's okay. Really, I can deal with it."

"No. For krat's sake, Jas, listen to yourself. The misborn assaulted you. You have to do something about it. You can't go through the rest of your life letting people push you around. You're in security," he exclaimed. "What are you going to do if you get attacked by aliens? Run away? Tell the people you're supposed to be protecting that you couldn't prove the aliens were attacking?"

"Hey," Jas replied defensively. "Of course I won't. I'll do my job. This is different."

"Not from where I'm sitting, it isn't."

Jas's lips thinned to a line. "I don't have a choice. I can't make waves. I can't afford to get kicked out of school. If I don't get through this, I'm not going to get another chance. I'm not like you. I can't just drift from college to college because I'm too lazy to do the work."

Sergei put down his fork and sat back, staring at Jas.

She closed her eyes. "Sorry. I didn't mean that the way it sounded."

He shook his head and resumed eating, silently.

Jas sighed. She reached out and took his hand. "I went over this with Tamara months ago. There really isn't anything I can do. I just have to suck it up and hope he doesn't teach any of my classes next year."

"You mean this has been going on for a while?"

"A little. Off and on."

Sergei looked at her gravely.

"Don't look at me like that. You don't get it. You're from Earth. You aren't different from everyone else. You don't stand out wherever you go. People aren't constantly asking about your background. They don't treat you differently. You're accepted for who you are. It isn't like that with me. To everyone else, I'm not Jas, I'm The Martian. Maybe the administration would believe me. I don't know. But I get too much attention as it is. I don't want any more."

"Jas, most people don't give a krat where you're from. This isn't the children's home," Sergei said. "Most people aren't like your instructor. You don't have to put up with his behavior."

Jas remembered being jumped in the stairwell by the children's home kids, having things thrown at the back of her head in class while the teacher's back was turned, and being the victim of subtle ostracizing. "Sergei, I know you think what you're saying is true, but you don't get it, and you never will. So let's just not talk about it, huh?"

He looked hurt, but he didn't press the issue. They tried to talk about other things, but their conversation was dry and forced. Ever since she'd told Sergei of her passion to travel the stars, a distance seemed to be developing between them that broke Jas's heart.

12

____

It was early summer, and the Great Antarctic Melt had begun. Every year, more and more of the deep layers of ice that covered and surrounded the continent were lost to the sea. In years past, massive icebergs had calved, shrinking and altering the shoreline, which in turn hastened the decimation of penguins and other species whose breeding strategies were dependent upon the landscape's stability. Freed of the weight of the ice, the landmass was rising to a higher elevation.

One element of the leadership skills class was regular excursions, when the students would conduct staged battles. Each team would try to defeat the others in order to attain a prize. Each team had a leader, and the rest of the team had to obey his or her orders. Afterward, the teams would analyze their leader's strategies as well as the reasons for their success or failure.

Everyone had taken their turn at playing the leader except for Jas and two others. The instructor had informed the class that they had one more opportunity for an excursion before the Melt made it impossible to travel over the ice.

When the evening of the final excursion that year arrived,

Clements assigned team members to Jas and the other leaders. They weren't allowed to choose their own teams. The instructor had pointed out in the beginning of the class that only rarely would they be able to choose who they would have working under them in real life.

As they prepared to set out to the battle site, Clements called out the team members. Sergei wasn't on Jas's team. She was sadly relieved. He went over to his leader while the four students she was to command that day approached her.

A transport took them a few kilometers away, out on the bare, windy landscape. Dusk was quickly falling. The vehicle stopped around four hundred meters from the ocean, where there were huge ice blocks for the students to hide behind. The blocks not only provided cover for the teams as they staged their battle, but they also offered variability in the routes to the target, which the leaders were supposed to figure into their strategies. The class had been at that place before, and by the time they alighted the transport Jas had already figured out what she thought was the best route to the prize.

She waited at the back of the line of students who were retrieving their packs from the underbelly of the vehicle. Their equipment consisted of suits of light-sensitive material in team colors and true laser guns. A beam of light from the weapons would register on the suits if it hit. They also had helmets they could communicate through.

Most of her team had retrieved their packs, and they were waiting for her on the other side of the vehicle. She couldn't see Sergei. Looking round, she saw he was right behind her. The students in front of Jas took their packs and left, and then it was just the two of them. Sergei touched her back, and a familiar spreading warmth and sweet ache radiated through her, dispelling the uncomfortable prickles that had been tickling her spine.

He leaned in for a brief kiss. "I love you," he murmured as

he drew back. She stood there in surprise while he took his pack and left, casting a smile at her over his shoulder.

Jas's mind spun. Sergei had never said those words to her. Why had he chosen there and then to tell her that?

She was slow getting her pack and joining the rest of her team. They had only minutes before the exercise began. Her team was looking at her expectantly. A short distance away on the uneven ground, Sergei stood with his group, toeing a shard of broken ice that was quickly melting to slush. The darkness was deepening by the minute.

She cleared her throat. "Okay, over there." She pointed to an outcrop that was far from their goal. She received some distrustful looks, but her team jogged over as she'd ordered. Clements was standing to one side, whistle in hand and checking the time.

They put on their light-sensitive suits. If a laser beam hit them, their suits would vibrate and sound an alarm. If they were hit in a vital part of the body, a 'death' alarm would sound, and they had to cease firing and stay where they were. A hit in a less-vulnerable spot would trigger a 'wound' alarm. After three wounds, they had to act as though dead. The suits recorded if any student disobeyed the rules.

Behind the outcrop, Jas drew the team together and explained her plan.

"But we're the furthest away," one of them complained. "The others will get there minutes before us."

"No, they won't," Jas said. "They're going to be fighting it out between them. If we stay at the back for a while, the others will take each other out along the way. They won't be firing at us. We can pick them off from behind. If we stay out of sight, they're going to think it's the other side who's firing, and they'll shoot at them, not us. When we've taken out the opposition as best we can, Richard can do his stuff."

Her team's expressions changed at her explanation.

"Okay," one said. "Let's do it."

The whistle blew, and the teams began to move. Almost immediately, an alarm sounded. Someone had tried to make a quick dash for the prize. The alarm was a high-pitched burst of sound. They'd been fatally hit. The 'dead' student sat down disconsolately. More students appeared briefly among the ice blocks. Another alarm sounded, and another. Wound alarms.

"Milas, go left," Jas said into her mic. She'd caught sight of a member of another team who had figured out her strategy. The student was doubling back to sneak up on them from behind. Milas hadn't seen the approaching student. He was running for cover, but he wouldn't make it. Jas lifted her gun to her shoulder to take aim. The high-pitched alarm sounded again, and the attacking student threw down his gun in anger. Someone had shot him. Jas glanced around to find Milas' savior. Sergei was behind her, pretending to blow smoke from the muzzle of his weapon.

What was he doing? He wasn't even on her team. "Why'd you do that?"

"You don't always have to play by the rules, Jas," he said.

She was vaguely annoyed. It was only a game, but if everyone messed around, no one would learn anything. She turned away, then immediately felt guilty. This was the man who loved her, and she loved him. She looked back to give him a smile, but he'd gone.

The other two teams were down to two people each. Milas' head popped out from around a chunk of ice. He shot and took out another student. Everyone was only fifty meters or so from the prize.

"Final stage," Jas said into her mic.

Richard started his run. He was the fastest of all of them. Jas knew where one of the other team members was, and she was waiting. As the woman peeped out, she shot her. A death alarm sounded, and the woman stood up. Richard was still running. A wound alarm rang out. Was he hit? Where was his assailant? Milas and another student rolled into view, throwing punches.

Another wound alarm. Someone was shooting at Richard. Jas desperately scanned the ice blocks in the deep twilight. Who was still left to shoot? Jas saw her. It was the smallest student, curled into a ball behind a small ice boulder that didn't look large enough to hide anyone.

Richard was almost at the prize. The small student raised her weapon to take another shot, and Jas fired. As Richard put his hand on the prize, two alarms sounded. Death alarms. Jas had hit the student square in the back. There was no doubt that she was dead. But had she managed to kill Richard before he'd gotten to the prize?

Everyone who was hiding revealed themselves, and the dead students stood up. Clements would tell them the outcome and give a brief breakdown of events before they completed a more thorough analysis the next morning.

As Jas was going over to join the others, a faint rumble seemed to come from nowhere. She paused, confused, and looked up. Was there a storm coming? The sky was starry and clear. The rumble grew louder. Vibration ran up Jas's legs, and she realized that the sound was coming from the ground.

The instructor was shouting, ordering them to run to the transport. Jas froze for a moment, wondering what was going on. The vibration got stronger, rocking her and almost throwing her off her feet. Then she understood. The ice they were standing on was breaking free of the land. They were on a newly calving, massive iceberg.

She sprinted for the vehicle, joining the other students who were speeding across the ice, slipping and stumbling in their haste. The driver had started the engine by the time they arrived. The students piled in. The instructor climbed aboard last, made a quick survey of the dark, empty landscape, and told the driver to go.

Most of the students hadn't had time to take seats. They were thrown backward into a jumble of bodies as the transport flew from the scene.

Jas was crushed against a window at the back. Behind them, a fissure yawned blackly in the shimmering surface. It quickly grew, exposing sheer walls of fresh ice. Jas's mouth fell open. The area where they'd just been standing was moving. It was crumbling, shifting. Millions of tons of ice was drifting, slipping away, out to sea. Huge waves rose up in the fissure and smashed down. A tidal wave of sea water rushed toward them, catching up to them even though the transport was tearing away from the scene. Jas's heart rose into her mouth.

The water seemed to rear up and reach out to the vehicle, but when it crashed down, it fell short. Only its feeble fingertips scrabbled at the transport's sleds.

Most of the other students had gotten into their seats while the scene was playing out behind them. They were oblivious to what had just happened. When Jas was unpinned from the window, she turned and saw Clements looking back, white-faced.

Jas found an empty seat and sat down, washed over with relief at their narrow escape. She took off her helmet and unzipped her suit. Her pulse began to slow, but something niggled at her. Something was wrong.

A terrible dread clutched her. She whipped around in her seat, looking for a face among the students in front and behind. Sergei. Where was Sergei?

13

____

Jas was in a starjump. She was nowhere. She didn't exist. She lay on her bed, unmoving. At times, Tamara came to her, talked to her, fed her. In between her friend's visits, sights and sounds entered her consciousness. The movements of her roommate, shadows that fell as she blocked the light. Noises from outside. Wind, and the hum of drones passing. Daylight filled the room, then darkness. Light, dark. How many times?

Jas was in a pit. She was at the bottom of a well, underwater. Somewhere above her, life carried on as normal, but she couldn't reach it. She couldn't climb out. Or was it that she didn't want to?

Murmuring in her room. "How long?" asked a voice. "It's been too long."

The college medic came. He checked her over, took her pulse, listened to her breathing, looked into her eyes, tested her reflexes. He asked her questions, but it was like he was speaking through wool. Jas heard the words, but as soon as she thought she understood, the meaning would slip away like threads of silk in the wind.

He left her. Pills arrived in Tamara's hands. She pushed Jas up, put them in her mouth, and made her drink water. She slept.

As she woke, she heard her roommate say, "She doesn't even cry. It's weird."

Jas opened her eyes. Tamara was there too. Jas moved, and her friend noticed. "Jas, you're awake," she said, coming over and squatting down. "How are you feeling?"

Her jaw muscles were strangely weak. "Groggy," Jas mumbled.

Tamara exhaled and touched Jas's head. "That's the first thing you've said in days."

Jas thought this information was probably significant, but she didn't know why.

"Becca and I were thinking it would be a good idea if we swapped rooms for the rest of the semester. I'll look after you until you're feeling better."

Was she sick? Yes, that had to be it. She had to be sick.

"Is that okay?" Tamara asked.

Jas forced her neck down, giving a slight nod.

It was weeks before she could mention the accident, and then she couldn't say his name. One evening, as Tamara was doing her homework and Jas was looking sightlessly out of the window, she said, "What happened after?"

"Hmm?" Tamara said absently. When Jas didn't reply, she looked up. She registered what Jas had said, and her face crumpled in sorrow. "Jas, I'm so sorry. After...after it happened, as soon as it was safe, you all went back to look for him. The police sent out a search party. They had boats out, and helis. Everyone looked for days. Don't you remember?"

Jas shook her head. "All I remember is..." The last thing she recalled was the tendrils of seawater slipping from the tracks of the transport and the dark, frozen landscape retreating behind her. That, and a figure of a man pretending to blow smoke from a gun. Then he was gone.

THE NEXT DAY, she got up and checked her interface for the classes she had that day. Battle tactics, weapons, survival, hand-to-hand. She went to take a shower, but Tamara was in the shower room. She waited outside until her friend came out, toweling her hair.

"You're up already?" Tamara asked. "Do you want some breakfast? I could make us both some. I still have time."

"No, I don't want any breakfast," Jas said as she went into the shower room.

"You've got to eat, Jas. You're wasting away to nothing."

"I'm fine," Jas said as she closed the door.

When she came out and started to get her things ready, Tamara asked, "You're going to class?"

"Yes, I've gotten really behind. How much have I missed? I don't know. It's been weeks."

"Jas, you don't have to. The college said you can repeat this semester on health grounds." She looked alarmed as she watched Jas push her interface into a bag along with her sports clothes. When she didn't stop, Tamara went over to her friend.

"Jas," she said, gently taking her bag from her. "Honestly, you don't have to go to class. It's okay."

Jas took her bag back. "I do have to go to class. I do."

She finished packing her bag. Then she put on her coat and hat and went out. She walked quickly, so that she was almost running. Something was inside her—something that squirmed like a damned soul trying to escape hell. If she could keep moving, if she could maintain focus, maybe she could prevent it from emerging and overwhelming her.

Eyes were upon her at her first class, but she barely noticed. Being a poor Martian and dealing with the attention her situation brought was nothing compared to what she now carried around inside her and would forever. She listened carefully and made extensive notes. A test was coming up next week. The final for that class. Had that much time passed? She could hardly believe it. She would have to catch up on the work. It would be hard, but she could do it. The same with the other subjects. She wouldn't skip the semester. She would graduate on schedule, and then she would leave on the first starship that would take her. If she left Antarctica far behind, maybe that would quiet the thing that writhed.

The morning flew by. Over lunch, Jas was fixated on her interface, hungrily devouring the information, but not her food. In the afternoon, she was a silent member of survival training while the rest of the class were discussing gathering water from the air in a desert.

Then came hand-to-hand combat. As usual, she stood at the back of the class, but Jas was the tallest person in the group. There was no way that Trankle could fail to notice her return. The first thing he said when he came into the training room was, "So Ms. Martian's here. Welcome back. Glad you're over your *illness*. Feeling better?"

Jas didn't answer. She fixed her gaze on the man.

He lifted his lip scornfully, turned to the other students and clapped his hands. "Last session of the year. Most of you have done pretty well. Some not so well. Today, we sort the wheat from the chaff. You know the drill. Five minutes per pair, on the mat, anything legal goes. Got it? Right. Who's first?"

Two students went to the mat. Trankle took out an interface and stood to the side. He nodded, and the students began to fight. Jas followed their motions, their blows and holds. They were pretty evenly matched. Had Trankle paired them up himself according to their fitness and ability? Who was her partner?

Trankle blew a whistle. The five minutes were up. He waved the students off the mat and made notes on his interface. Another pair took their place and a moment later they too began to fight. A third pair replaced them, and a fourth. The process was efficient. Trankle gave no indication whether a student had passed or failed.

Finally, all the students had fought. Only Jas was left, and as the class was an odd number, there was no one to partner her. The students were standing around, waiting to be dismissed. The final pair to fight were panting and sweating.

Trankle completed his notes, smiled to himself, closed the interface, and put it down in a corner of the room. He returned to the center, folded his arms, and rocked on his heels, a small smile still playing around his lips.

"Looks like there's no one left to fight with our Martian. Shame, but it doesn't really matter. You've missed so many classes, Harrington, you've already failed."

"Huh?" Jas said. "No. I just have to pass the test. It doesn't matter how much I've missed. I have a health exemption."

Trankle shook his head. "My class, my rules. And I don't accept health exemptions."

He was lying. She knew it. "I want to fight."

"I've just told you, you can't. The course is over. Class dismissed."

Jas didn't move. "I want to fight."

"Give her a chance," a male student said. "I'll fight again. I'll fight you, Jas."

"Yeah, give her a chance," a few more students echoed.

Trankle snorted. "You just don't know when to give up, do

you?" he said to Jas. "Right. So you want to fight? You can fight me. Come on. Let's do it." He backed up until he was on the training mat.

Jas didn't hesitate. The thing inside drove her. She ran at her tormentor, taking him by surprise. At the last second, she jumped and kicked him in the stomach. Trankle tried to block her foot, but she was too fast for him. Her heel sank into his abdomen, and if the man hadn't been well-muscled, that would have been the end of the fight.

He doubled over and staggered back, his face red and contorted. Jas raised her foot again to deliver a kick to his head, but Trankle just managed to catch her calf before the blow connected. They struggled for a moment, Trankle still bent over, one arm over his stomach and the other hand gripping Jas's leg. She hopped and tugged, trying to free her foot.

The instructor regained a little breath and immediately expended it in a cry of rage. This seemed to galvanize Jas, and instead of trying to get away from Trankle, she hopped closer and brought down a fist on the back of his head. The man fell forward. His grip on Jas's ankle broke. He hadn't even reached the mat before she kicked his head, snapping it to the side. With a dull thunk and a loud exhale, he hit the floor.

Jas drew back her leg to kick him again, but hands were restraining her, pulling her away. When she stopped struggling, the hands let go. She was vaguely aware of pain radiating from her foot. She stared at the unconscious Trankle, hardly knowing what she'd done.

For that moment at least, the thing inside was quiet.

THE YEAR WAS OVER. Tamara was packing, getting ready to catch the autobus that would take her to the spaceport.

"Jas, my offer still stands. Why won't you come home with me for the long vacation? My dad really won't mind."

Jas shook her head. "I'll miss your cooking, but I'll be fine right here. I found a place in town to stay while I catch up on my studies."

"But you passed everything. Why do you need to study?"

"I *scraped* all my passes. If I don't catch up on what I missed, I'm only going to find everything harder next year."

"But what if you run out of creds? Are you sure you have enough?"

"I'll find a job. It's tourist season. There has to be some casual work around. I'll be okay."

"But..." Tamara sighed. "I'm not going to persuade you, am I?"

"Sorry. But I'm really going to be fine. I promise. Now that I don't have that inquiry into my fight with Trankle hanging over me, I just want to get my head down and work."

"Yeah, that was sweet how all the students said it was a fair fight, wasn't it?"

Jas chuckled. "I bet he'll wear his safety gear next time he decides to do some sparring."

"Huh, yeah. Well, keep in touch, right?" She zipped up her case and went to give Jas a hug.

When Tamara had gone, Jas started her own packing. She didn't have many things, so it didn't take her long. When she'd finished, she took a final look at the room. She recalled Aggy's sullen face as she'd talked with her boyfriend on her interface, and Becca, who Jas hadn't gotten to know very well. Last, she remembered kind, loyal Tamara, who had cared for her when she was at her lowest.

Someone else had also spent many nights in that room with her, but she skirted around the memory. She wasn't ready to go there yet.

In another two years, she would be saying goodbye to the

McMurdo Sound Training Institute for the last time. At that thought, she climbed onto her bare mattress so that she could look out of the window and into the sky. A whole galaxy was open to her. She wondered where she would go and what she would find there.